Penny and the Four Questions

by Nancy E. Krulik
Illustrated by Marian Young

SCHOLASTIC INC.
New York Toronto London Sydney Auckland

For Amanda Elizabeth Burwasser: the next generation
to ask the four questions
—N.K.

To Denny, Saskia, and Rodney
—M.Y.

ISBN 0-590-46339-X

12 11 10 9 8 7 6 5 4 3 5 6 7 8/9

Printed in the U.S.A. 24

First Scholastic printing, March 1993

Note to the Reader:

In ancient times, the Jewish people lived in Egypt as slaves. During the seder, we tell the story of how we escaped from Egypt and from slavery. The four questions remind us of that time and they remind us to be grateful that we are free today.

—N.K.

WHY IS THIS NIGHT DIFFERENT FROM ALL OTHER NIGHTS?
THE FOUR QUESTIONS:

On all other nights we eat either leavened bread or unleavened; on this night why do we eat only unleavened bread?
When the Jews ran away from their Egyptian slave masters, they had no time to wait for their bread to rise. They had to take unleavened bread with them.

On all other nights we eat herbs of any kind; on this night why do we eat only bitter herbs?
The bitter herbs remind us of the bitterness of slavery.

On all other nights we do not dip our herbs even once; on this night why do we dip them twice?
We dip the herbs in salt water to remind us of the tears of the Jewish slaves.

On all other nights we eat our meals in any manner; on this night why do we sit around the table together in a reclining position?
As slaves, the Jews were not allowed to sit comfortably and enjoy dinner. But as free people, today's Jews can eat and relax.

"How much longer until the seder, Mommy?"
"Only one more hour, Penny. Be patient!"

Be patient, be patient. That's all Mommy ever says to me. I'm not very good at being patient. And today it's worse than ever! Tonight's seder isn't going to be just *any* Passover dinner! Tonight, I will ask the four questions for the very first time!

When you say the four questions you are asking why the first night of Passover is different from all other nights. Usually, the youngest child at the table gets to ask the questions. Up until now, my brother Jeffrey has gotten to ask them. That's because he could read Hebrew and I couldn't.

But this year, I've been going to Hebrew school. Now I can read Hebrew, too! So tonight, I am going to read the four questions in front of everyone—Jeffrey, Mommy, Daddy, Grandma, and Grandpa!

"Mommy, what time is it *now*?"

"Five minutes later than it was the last time you asked!" Mommy laughs. "Here, help me with the seder plate. That will make the time move faster!"

I love helping Mommy get ready for Passover. First, she gets down the big seder plate. We fill it with the special holiday foods: roasted egg, bitter herbs, a shank bone, horse radish, and apples and nuts. We set the seder plate in the middle of the table where everyone can see it.

Then Mommy takes three matzohs out of the box and puts them next to Daddy's chair. The middle matzoh is called the *afikomen*. I love the *afikomen*. At the beginning of the meal, Daddy hides it. I have to find it. If I do, I get a prize. I guess Daddy wants me to get a prize because every year he hides the *afikomen* in the same place—inside his napkin!

I get to help set the table. I put a plate at each chair. One for Mommy, one for Daddy, one for Jeffrey, one for me, one for Grandma, and one for Grandpa....

But there are three extra chairs at the table.

"Mommy, you set too many places."

"No I didn't, sweetie. I've invited another family to our seder. They just moved here from Russia. This will be their very first seder.

"Best of all, they have a little girl, too. Her name is Natasha. She's seven, just a year younger than you."

Younger than I am! Oh, no! What if she can read Hebrew?

"Mommy, I can still read the four questions tonight, can't I?" I ask quickly.

I don't like the look on Mommy's face at all! Something tells me Natasha is learning to read Hebrew, too.

Mommy bends down and looks me right in the eye. "Penny, Natasha and her family have never been to a seder before. This will be a very important night for them. Natasha has been working really hard to learn enough Hebrew to read the four questions at her very first seder. Please let her ask the questions tonight. You can say the four questions at the seder tomorrow night."

Tomorrow night! *Tomorrow night!* What's so great about tomorrow night? Tomorrow night Grandma and Grandpa will be at a different seder. They will have to wait a whole year to hear me ask the four questions!

Mommy sends me upstairs to get dressed for the seder. I was going to wear my new blue sailor dress, but now I'm not. That dress was for a special occasion. But this seder isn't going to be special anymore. I'll wear my green dress instead.

I hear the doorbell ring. Grandma and Grandpa are here! I'm so excited I almost forget to be angry about Natasha. I run down the stairs as fast as I can. Grandpa is right there to catch me.

"Happy Passover, Penny."

"Happy Passover, Grandpa. Happy Passover, Grandma."

Then they each bend over and give me a kiss on the cheek. We're a Penny sandwich!

When the doorbell rings again, Jeffrey runs to open the door. My brother is very excited about our Russian guests. Why shouldn't he be? It wasn't *his* turn to ask the four questions tonight!

Natasha's mother has a big bouquet of yellow tulips for my mommy. I love tulips. When I see them I know spring is finally here. While I am smelling Mommy's flowers, Natasha shyly walks up to me and places a package in my hand.

"Here. This is for you," she says slowly.

Wow! This means I will get two presents tonight—one for the *afikomen* and one from Natasha! I tear open the box.

Inside is a large, round, wooden doll with bright red flowers painted on her dress. A yellow and green kerchief is painted on her head.

"I've never seen a doll like this," I tell Natasha.

Natasha takes the doll out of my hand. With a flick of her wrist she twists the doll in half. Inside is another doll. Natasha twists that doll in half. And inside *that* doll is still another!

"I have a doll just like this at home," Natasha explains. "It was the only toy I could bring to America with me."

Her only toy! Suddenly I think of all of the dolls, toy trucks, and stuffed animals sitting in my room. I can't imagine having to choose just one to keep.

"Okay, everybody, let's start the seder!" Daddy says. We all follow him into the dining room.

Daddy sits at the head of the table. He puts a big pillow behind his head.

"We are supposed to be comfortable and relaxed at the seder," he explains to Natasha.

"Just don't fall asleep before I get my *afikomen* prize!" I tell him.

"Mmmm...dinner smells delicious!" Natasha's father says.

"We're having matzoh ball soup, turkey with farfel stuffing, carrots, and sweet potatoes!" Jeffrey announces. "Hurry with the seder, Dad. I'm hungry!"

Jeffrey is always hungry!

"So much food," Natasha's mother says with amazement. "In Moscow we had to wait on long lines just to get a loaf of bread or a piece of meat. Sometimes you waited on line all morning. And when you got into the store there was nothing left. I am so glad we live here in America now."

I think about yesterday when I went to the supermarket with Mommy and Daddy to buy our Passover food. There was plenty of food. And we didn't have to wait on any lines at all.

"It was very kind of you to invite us to your seder," Natasha's father says. "For so many years we could not observe the Jewish holidays. This is the first holiday we have ever celebrated."

No Jewish holidays! I can't believe it. That means Natasha has never had apples and honey on Rosh Hashanah or lit the candles on the Sabbath or gotten presents for Hanukkah. Mommy is right—Natasha should say the four questions. Tonight is more special for her than it is for me.

I smile at Mommy. I want her to know it is okay with me if Natasha says the four questions.

Mommy smiles back at me across the table. She always knows what I am smiling about.

Daddy opens up the *Haggadah*, a special prayer book we read only on Passover. He starts to pray in Hebrew. Daddy is reading much faster than I can follow in the *Haggadah*. So I close my eyes and listen to him.

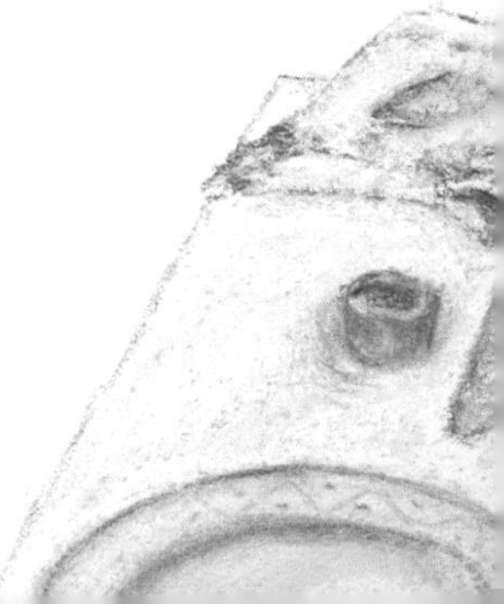

It doesn't take long to reach the part of the service when we read the four questions.

"Okay, Natasha, it's your turn," Daddy says.

Natasha stands up. Her hands are shaking. I can tell she is really scared.

"*Mahnishtanah halayla hazeh*," she says in Hebrew.

I wait for Natasha to go on, but she doesn't.

"I am having trouble," Natasha says. She looks as if she is going to cry.

I stand up next to Natasha and take her hand.

"Don't cry. I'll say it with you," I tell her. "We'll do it together."

Together, Natasha and I ask the four questions. We say them in Hebrew and we don't make any mistakes.

When we finish, everyone applauds—even Jeffrey! Natasha and I sit down. We hold hands under the table. That's the kind of thing best friends do.

Soon Daddy goes out of the room to wash his hands.

"Now's your chance," I tell Natasha. "You have to find the *afikomen*, so you can get your prize."

"But where is it?" Natasha says. She starts looking under the table and behind the chairs.

"Check inside Daddy's napkin," I whisper to her. "He always keeps it there!"

Natasha grabs the *afikomen* from Daddy's napkin and holds it up.

"Now you will get the prize at the end of the seder," I tell her.

"But you told me where it was. The prize should be yours," Natasha says.

"I have a better idea," I say. Then I whisper my idea into her ear.

All through the seder I let Natasha keep the *afikomen*. Then, after the meal, we both give it back to Daddy. Daddy reaches behind his chair and hands us our gift.

At first I let Natasha tear open the wrapping paper. But she takes too long. So I reach over and help her. With one good yank, I rip open the package.

It's a coloring book with a box of crayons! What a great prize! Natasha and I can color in all the pictures—together. Because *that* is what best friends do!